# Marvin's Invention

by Dina Anastasio • illustrated by Ann Iosa

Printed in Italy ISBN 0-948936-71-1

Cousin Marvin came to visit. He said hello to everyone, and then he went into his room.

Marvin put his suitcase on the bed and began
to unpack. Marvin's suitcase was filled with pieces
of metal and strange round shapes.

4

"What's all that?" Timmy asked.
"It's my latest invention," Marvin said.
"What does it do?" Timmy asked.
"You'll see," Marvin told him.

The next morning Timmy and his family cleaned the house. Marvin stayed in his room and worked on his invention.

That afternoon Timmy and his family went to
the cinema. Marvin stayed at home and worked on
his invention.

When they came home, Penny tried to open the front door, but the doorknob was missing.

"I'm sure the doorknob was here when we left," said Daddy.

Everyone nodded in agreement.

Timmy knocked on the door, but no one answered. Penny rang the bell.

"Marvin must be so busy working on his invention that he can't hear us," said Penny.

"Timmy," said Daddy "will you climb through the window and open the door for us?"

"Of course," said Timmy. "Just give me a push."

9

Soon everyone was inside. Penny went into her room and turned on her radio. Nothing happened. Penny picked up her radio and shook it. The insides were gone. Someone had taken all the wires out.

Penny ran into the sitting room.

"Did you take the insides of my radio?" she asked Timmy.

"Of course not," answered Timmy. "Why would I do that?"

"Well," said Penny. "They've disappeared."

"Please don't argue, children," said Daddy, as he went off to the bathroom.

"I'm going to have my bath. We'll solve this problem later."

"Yes," said Mummy. "We'll all help find the insides of your radio in a little while. Right now, I want to watch the six-o'clock news. Timmy, dear," she said. "Is it six o'clock yet?"

13

Timmy ran into his room to look at his alarm clock, but it wasn't there.

"Is it six yet?" Mummy shouted.

"I don't know," Timmy said. "Someone has taken my alarm clock."

"That's strange," Mummy said. "Maybe Daddy knows where it is."

Timmy knocked on the bathroom door.
"Daddy!" he said. "Have you seen my
alarm clock?"

"I haven't seen your alarm clock." he said.
"Have you seen my soap?"

Daddy put on his bathrobe and followed Timmy
into the sitting room.

"Something very strange is going on around here," Daddy said. "My soap is missing. Timmy's alarm clock is missing."

"And someone has taken the insides of my radio," Penny added.

"Let's watch the news," Mummy said. "We'll find everything later."

Daddy turned on the television.

"No, no" Mummy said. "That's the wrong channel. Change the channel."

"I can't," Daddy said. "The dial is missing."

Just then Marvin appeared in the doorway.

19

"Excuse me," Marvin said, "but I'd like you
to meet my invention."

Mummy pointed to the middle of Marvin's
invention.

"Isn't that the missing TV dial?" she asked.
"What does your invention do?" Timmy asked.
"Just turn the dial and you'll see," Marvin said.

Timmy turned the dial. The invention blew a great big bubble. Then it blew another bubble, and another bubble, and another bubble, until the sitting room was filled with bubbles.

"Turn if OFF!" cried Mummy.
"Hmmm," said Daddy, "I wonder if that's what happened to my soap."

Marvin turned the dial.

Marvin's invention started to sing. It sang "Pop Goes the Weasel" and "Three Blind Mice." It sang old songs and new songs. It sang and sang and sang. It sang louder and louder.

"Turn it OFF!" Daddy shouted.
"Maybe that's what happened to the insides of my radio," Penny said.

25

Marvin turned the dial again. The invention started to ring.

"That sounds like my alarm clock," Timmy said.

The invention rang and rang and rang.

"It must be six o'clock," Timmy said.
"I set the alarm for six o'clock."
"It's time for the news," Mummy said.

Mummy walked over to the invention, pulled off the dial, and put it back on the TV.

"I hope you don't mind," she said to Marvin. "But I need this to watch the news."

"That's all right," said Marvin.

Baby walked behind the invention and pointed.
"Look!" she said.
Daddy looked at the back of the invention.
"Well, well," he said. "So that's what happened
to our doorknob."

Daddy turned the doorknob and opened the back of the invention. He reached inside and pulled out the insides of Penny's radio.

"I hope you don't mind, Marvin," Daddy said, "but Penny wants to listen to her radio."

"That's all right," said Marvin.

Then Daddy pulled out Timmy's alarm clock and a bar of soap. The soap had almost melted.

"Timmy needs his clock to tell time, and I need what's left of the soap to have my bath," said Daddy. Then he put the doorknob back on the door.

"Marvin," Daddy said, "I think the best place for your invention is in your room. I hope you don't mind."

Marvin didn't mind a bit. He took his invention
upstairs and got right to work—on a brand new,
super-special surprise.